JUN 0 3 2021

THE GROSS HUMAN BODY IN ACTION
AUGMENTED REALITY

MUSCLES and BONES

A Repulsive AUGMENTED REALITY Experience

Gillia M. Olson

Lerner Publications ◆ Minneapolis

EXPLORE THE HUMAN BODY IN BRAND-NEW WAYS WITH AUGMENTED REALITY!

1. Ask a parent or guardian for permission to download the free Lerner AR app on your digital device by going to the App Store or Google Play. When you launch the app, choose the Gross Human Body series.

2. As you read, look for this icon throughout the book. It means there is an augmented reality experience on that page!

3. Use the Lerner AR app to scan the picture near the icon.

4. Watch the human body's systems come alive with augmented reality!

CONTENTS

INTRODUCTION
THE HUMAN MEAT SUIT

Your body is a meat suit. People are made of meat. Most of that meat is muscle, and skin covers your muscles. If it didn't, you'd look like a bunch of raw steaks.

Bones and muscles work together every time you move your body.

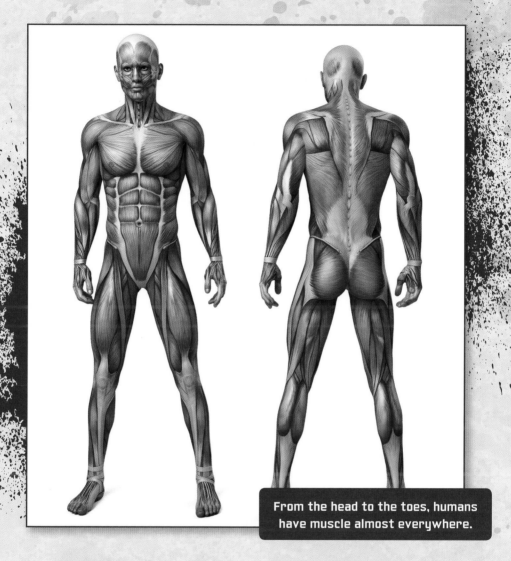

From the head to the toes, humans have muscle almost everywhere.

   Your bones keep you from flopping around like a meat-filled sack. Jellyfish, worms, and other animals without bones are cool in their own squishy ways, but you wouldn't want to look like them. Our skeletons make us part of an elite group. Only about 4 percent of animals have skeletons. Let's get to know our bones and the meat suits hanging on them.

CHAPTER 1

SQUISHY BONES: MAKING BLOOD

Bones might seem hard and solid. The outside of a bone is thick and hard. It's called cortical bone. But the inside is meaty and flexible. It's made up of spongy trabecular bone, the kind of bone that holds marrow.

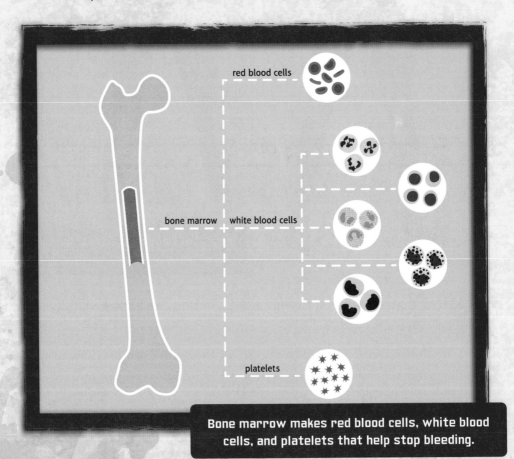

red blood cells

bone marrow   white blood cells

platelets

Bone marrow makes red blood cells, white blood cells, and platelets that help stop bleeding.

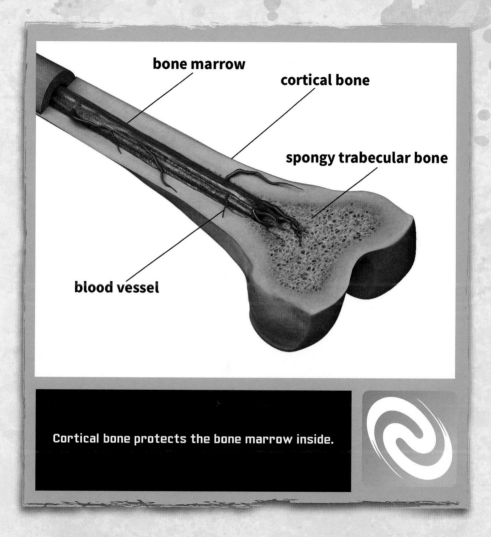

bone marrow

cortical bone

spongy trabecular bone

blood vessel

Cortical bone protects the bone marrow inside.

Bone marrow can be red or yellow. Red bone marrow makes blood cells. That's right—your bones make the blood that flows through your body and oozes out when you cut your skin. Marrow becomes yellow as you age. Yellow bone marrow stores fat. In an adult's thigh bone, or femur, you'll find red at the ends and yellow in the middle.

Babies are born with about 300 bones. At the ends of each bone are sections of flexible cartilage called growth plates. As kids get older, many of their bones grow and fuse together. You're probably losing bones right now! When you're done growing, your growth plates harden and become bone. Adults usually end up with 206 bones.

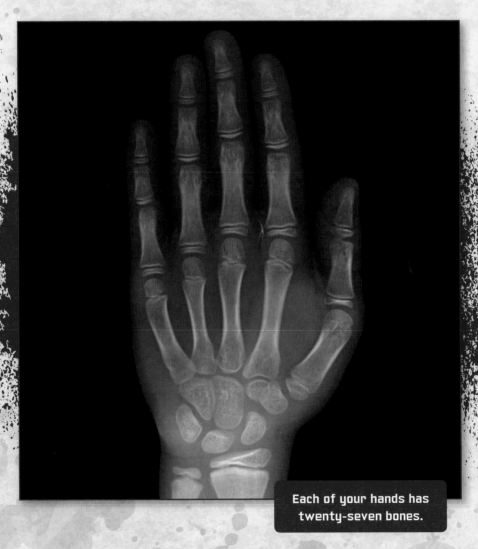

Each of your hands has twenty-seven bones.

The femur's head fits into a socket in your hip.

Bones come in many shapes and sizes. Picture the long bones with knobs at the ends that dogs like to chew on. That's what your femur looks like. Short bones often look like cubes or rocks. You can find a lot of short bones in your hands and feet. Flat bones such as your shoulder blades are thin and flat. Many of the bones that make up your skull are flat bones.

LET'S GET CRACKING: BROKEN BONES

Bones are strong. One cubic inch (16 cu. cm) of bone can withstand the weight of five pickup trucks before cracking. But bones can break, or fracture, in a bunch of nasty, painful ways.

Bone breaks can be closed or open. Open, or compound, breaks occur when the skin splits open near the fracture. The bloody wound is usually caused by broken bone cutting the skin. Ouch!

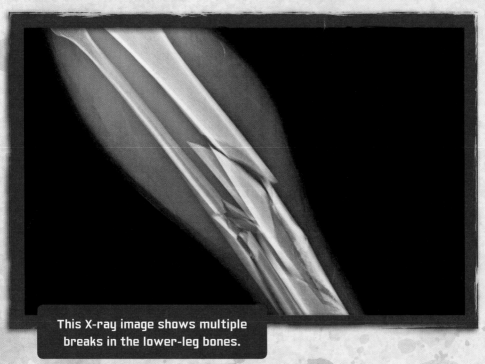

This X-ray image shows multiple breaks in the lower-leg bones.

Your femurs are the strongest bones in your body, but they can break if enough force is applied to them.

Closed fractures don't cut through the skin. They might be large or as thin as a hair. Stress fractures are small bone cracks caused by doing the same thing over and over, such as running or jumping.

Sometimes bones have a clean break, such as a single snap or crack. Other times, a bone might break in several places. Bone pieces may end up in your muscles and skin. Greenstick breaks are named for the way flexible tree branches break. The bone stretches and cracks on one side.

A cast supports and protects a broken bone, allowing it to heal.

Broken bones usually heal quickly. But some people are born with bone diseases that are harder, or even impossible, to treat. Brittle bone disease makes bones fragile and easily broken. Stone man syndrome affects muscles and other tissues in the body, slowly turning them to bone. Proteus syndrome causes skin, bones, and muscles to overgrow. It can create large tumors of skin and bone. Luckily, conditions such as these are rare.

Much more common are conditions such as rheumatoid arthritis. It's an immune system disorder that attacks the lining of the joints, causing pain and damage. Osteoarthritis is caused by cartilage between bones wearing away over time. Eventually, the condition causes bone to rub on bone. Osteoporosis makes bones thin and easily broken. It's most common in older people.

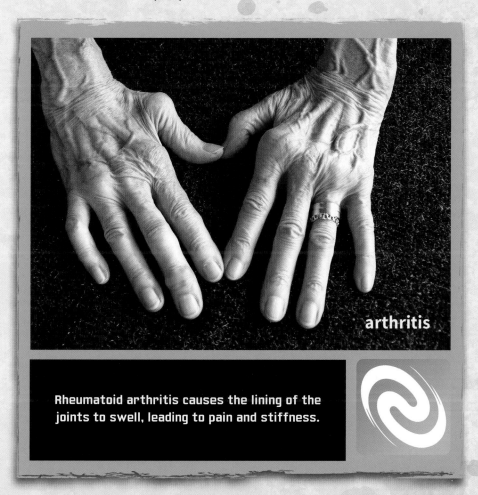

arthritis

Rheumatoid arthritis causes the lining of the joints to swell, leading to pain and stiffness.

BONE CUSHIONS AND BLOOD PUMPERS: MEATY MUSCLES

Muscles are meat. If you want to know what your muscles look like, check out raw chicken or steak. When people eat meat, they are usually eating animal muscle.

Bones can't move by themselves. Your muscles move your bones so you can run, dance, and swim. Muscles also protect bones and organs by providing padding against bumps and jolts.

Humans have three main types of muscles: skeletal, smooth, and cardiac. Skeletal muscles attach to your bones.

White meat, such as a chicken breast, is slow-twitch muscle.

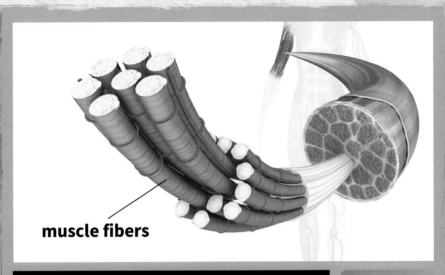

muscle fibers

The biceps muscle in your upper arm is made of mostly fast-twitch muscle fibers.

You control skeletal muscles when you move, but there's one thing they do without your control: they shiver when you're cold. The rapid muscle movement produces heat that helps keep you warm.

Skeletal muscles can be slow twitch or fast twitch. Pink fast-twitch muscle fibers provide short bursts of speed. Slow-twitch fibers look red because they carry a lot of oxygen-rich blood, which is better for slower, longer movements. Think of fast-twitch muscles for sprints and slow-twitch muscles for marathons.

Your head contains a bunch of amazing skeletal muscles. Some of the busiest ones are around your eyes. Six muscles control each eye. In one hour of reading, your eyes can make ten thousand movements.

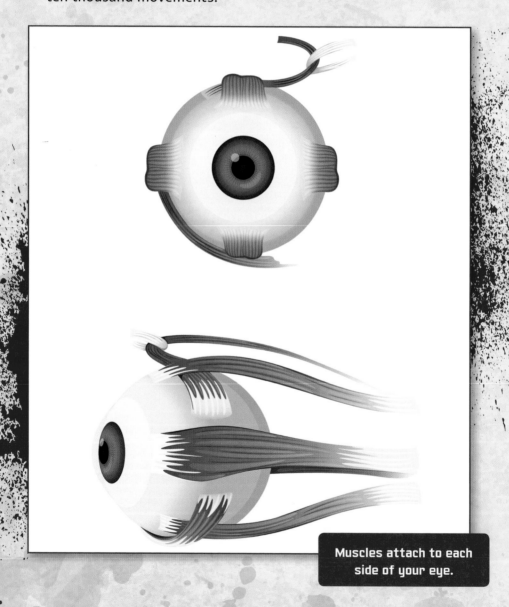

Muscles attach to each side of your eye.

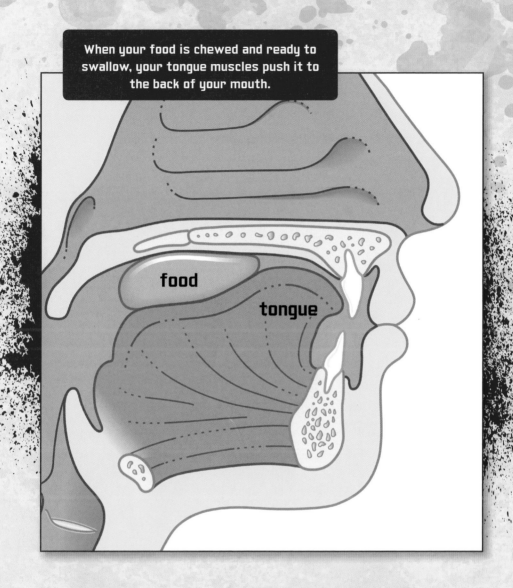

When your food is chewed and ready to swallow, your tongue muscles push it to the back of your mouth.

food

tongue

Your tongue is made up of eight muscles that work together like an octopus's arm. Your tongue muscles are the only muscles you control that aren't connected to bone at both ends. The masseter muscles in your jaw are some of the strongest muscles in your body. They help you to bite down with a force of 200 pounds (91 kg).

Smooth muscle is not attached to bone. It's the weakest type of muscle, but it does a lot of work. Smooth muscles line the inside of blood vessels and organs, helping blood flow and food move through your body.

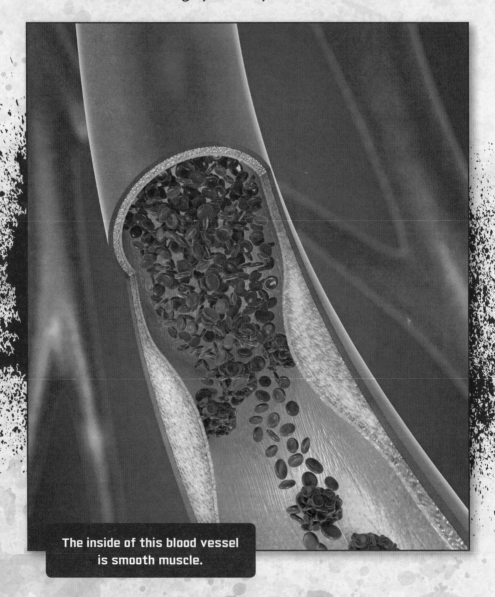

The inside of this blood vessel is smooth muscle.

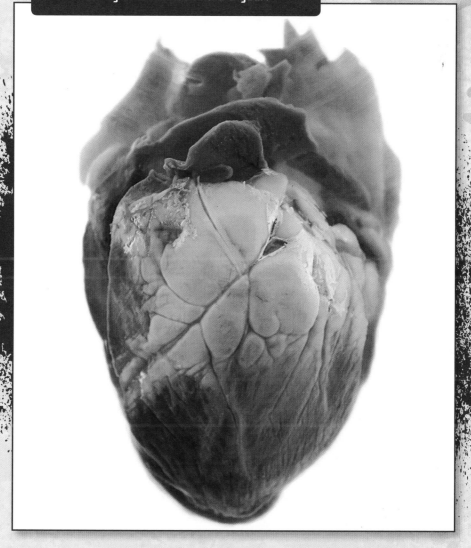

Cardiac muscle is found in your heart. It pumps blood throughout your body. Like smooth muscle, cardiac muscle works without your having to think about it—thank goodness! Your heart pumps about 2,000 gallons (7,570 L) of blood a day.

CHAPTER 4

CRAMPS, RIPS, AND STRAINS: MUSCLE PROBLEMS

Have you felt your eyelid twitch? When you're falling asleep, do you ever suddenly wake up with a jerk? Muscle twitches happen when nerves and muscles fire off on their own, and scientists don't always know why. When you're about to fall asleep, your muscles relax, which might trick your brain into thinking you're falling. Your brain jerks you awake.

Eyelid twitches can be caused by stress, too much caffeine, and not enough sleep.

Using a keyboard without taking
breaks may cause cramps.

Cramps are unconscious movements that can hurt. Cramps
happen when your muscles squeeze without your controlling
them. Overusing muscles, drinking not enough water, and
holding muscles in one position for a long time can cause
cramps. Writer's cramp can affect your hand when you use
a pen or pencil for a long time. A charley horse is a common
type of cramp caused by a strain or bruise. Any muscle can
experience a charley horse, but it's most common in your legs.

Everyone has muscle pain from time to time. It happens when you overwork your muscles. During a heavy workout, you make little tears in your muscle tissue. When you sleep, your body repairs the tissue, making it bigger than before the workout. You know what they say—no pain, no gain!

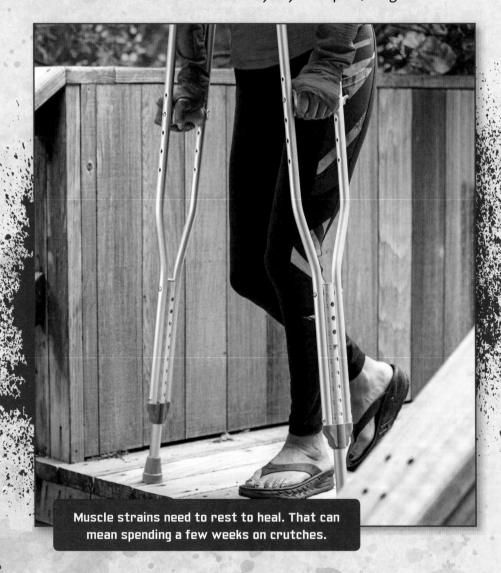

Muscle strains need to rest to heal. That can mean spending a few weeks on crutches.

A doctor performs surgery to repair a patient's knee ligament. Some sprains heal on their own, but more severe sprains require surgery.

Sometimes people strain muscles. It can happen when muscle fibers stretch or tear too much. Strains hurt and need time to rest and heal.

Other body tissue can also become injured. Tendons connect muscles to bones. They can get strained, similar to the way muscles overstretch and tear. Ligaments connect bones to other bones. Sprained ligaments are stretched, twisted, or torn.

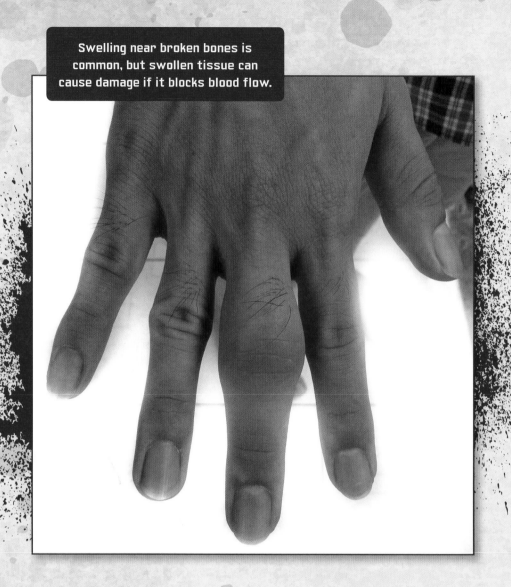

Swelling near broken bones is common, but swollen tissue can cause damage if it blocks blood flow.

Sometimes a broken bone causes muscle damage. When muscles and bones are injured, fluid can build up in the area. Tissue near the injury holds in the fluid, squeezing blood vessels until blood flow stops. To avoid permanent muscle damage, doctors may have to cut open the tissue to drain the fluid. Fun!

Tetanus is a disease caused by bacteria that get into the body through a cut or burn. The disease makes your muscles tighten, including your masseters. This forces your jaw to clamp shut. That's why tetanus is also called lockjaw. People get tetanus shots to avoid this painful disease.

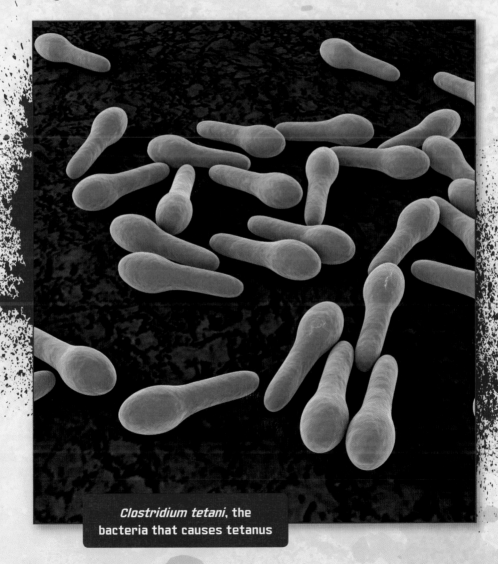

Clostridium tetani, the bacteria that causes tetanus

Other bacteria can cause super-gross problems. Flesh-eating bacteria eat muscles. These bacteria are hard to treat, so the affected tissue needs to be removed before the bacteria spreads. Some people end up losing their legs or arms.

People who lose body parts to flesh-eating bacteria might replace them with artificial parts. Luckily, such cases are extremely rare.

When your muscles and bones are healthy, they help you do all kinds of fun things.

Parasites can affect muscles too. Malaria is a parasite that attacks oxygen-carrying red blood cells. The lack of oxygen caused by malaria creates muscle pain. Trichinosis is an infection caused by parasitic roundworms. Roundworm larvae get into the body through undercooked meat and grow into adult roundworms in the intestine. They travel through muscles and cause fever, muscle pain, and vomiting.

Diseases, parasites, and injuries can be gross and scary, but don't worry. Most of the time, your muscles and bones do a good job of keeping you safe. They let you dance, kick, and read this book! Be nice to your meat suit, and it will usually take care of you.

GROSS MUSCLE AND BONE FACTS

- The biggest and heaviest muscle in your body is the gluteus maximus—the main muscle in your rear end.

- Your smallest muscle is in your ear. The stapedius moves a bone that helps control sound vibration.

- People sometimes eat the bone marrow of cows, lambs, and other animals. When it's cooked, bone marrow tastes similar to butter.

- Some people have more than 206 bones. About 1 percent of people are born with an extra rib above their collarbone.

- About 85 percent of the heat in your body is produced by muscle movement.

- Muscles make up about 30 to 40 percent of the average person's weight.

GLOSSARY

bacteria: tiny living things that live all around and inside you

blood vessel: a tube through which blood circulates in the body

bone marrow: a soft tissue inside most bones where blood cells form

cartilage: a flexible tissue in the body

immune system: the system that protects the body against disease and infection

ligament: a tough band connecting bones or supporting an organ in place

muscle fiber: any of the long cells that make up muscle

parasite: a living thing that lives in or on another living thing

sprain: the stretching or tearing of a ligament

strain: the stretching or tearing of a tendon or muscle

tendon: a tough cord or band that connects a muscle with another body part

FURTHER INFORMATION

Bennett, Howard J. *The Fantastic Body: What Makes You Tick & How You Get Sick*. Emmaus, PA: Rodale Kids, 2017.

Biology for Kids: Bacteria
https://www.ducksters.com/science/bacteria.php

Duhaime, Darla. *Gross Body Stuff*. Vero Beach, FL: Rourke Educational Media, 2016.

Farndon, John. *Stickmen's Guide to Your Mighty Muscles and Bones*. Minneapolis: Hungry Tomato, 2018.

Muscles
https://www.pbslearningmedia.org/resource/muscles-science-trek/muscles-science-trek/

Muscular System
https://www.innerbody.com/image/musfov.html

Rose, Simon. *Skeletal System*. New York: AV2 by Weigl, 2020.

Your Bones
https://kidshealth.org/en/kids/bones.html

INDEX

PHOTO ACKNOWLEDGMENTS

Image credits: master1305/iStock/Getty Images, p. 4; SEBASTIAN KAULITZKI/
SCIENCE PHOTO LIBRARY/Getty Images, p. 5; stockdevil/iStock/Getty Images,
p. 6; Science Picture Company/Getty Images, p. 7; WichienTep/iStock/Getty
Images, p. 8; Drbouz/Getty Images, p. 9; thesleepless1/iStock/Getty Images, p. 10;
yodiyim/Getty Images, p. 11; Westend61/Getty Images, p. 12; StanRohrer/Getty
Images, p. 13; Tetra Images/Getty Images, p. 14; 7activestudio/Getty Images,
p. 15; blueringmedia/iStock/Getty Images, p. 16; Dorling Kindersley/Getty Images,
p. 17; CHRISTOPH BURGSTEDT/SCIENCE PHOTO LIBRARY/Getty Images, p. 18;
MAIKA 777/Getty Images, p. 19; jaojormami/Shutterstock.com, p. 20; krisanapong
detraphiphat/Getty Images, p. 21; Bill Oxford/iStock/Getty Images, p. 22;
RaulTopan/iStock/Getty Images, p. 23; Boonmee Plangdee/EyeEm/Getty Images,
p. 24; KATERYNA KON/SCIENCE PHOTO LIBRARY/Getty Images, p. 25; UpperCut
Images/Getty Images, p. 26; Annie Otzen/Getty Images, p. 27. AR Experience:
TurboSquid, Inc. Design elements: EduardHarkonen/Getty Images; atakan/
Getty Images; kaylabutler/Getty Images; Eratel/Getty Images; gadost/Getty
Images; Freer/Shutterstock.com; Anastasiia_M/Getty Images (green slime frame);
Anastasiia_M/Getty Images (green slime blot); amtitus/Getty Images; desifoto/
Getty Images; Yevhenii Dubinko/Getty Images; arthobbit/Getty Images; cajoer/
Getty Images; enjoynz/Getty Images.

Cover images: decade3d/iStock/Getty Images; jakkapan21/iStock/Getty Images;
tonaquatic/iStock/Getty Images.

Lerner Publications Company
An imprint of Lerner Publishing Group, Inc.
241 First Avenue North
Minneapolis, MN 55401 USA

For reading levels and more information, look up this title at www.lernerbooks.com.

Main body text set in Aptifer Sans LT Pro.
Typeface provided by Linotype AG.

Designer: Kimberly Morales

Library of Congress Cataloging-in-Publication Data

Names: Olson, Gillia M., author.
Title: Bones and muscles : a repulsive augmented reality experience / Gillia M. Olson.
Description: Minneapolis : Lerner Publications, [2021] | Series: The gross human body in action: augmented reality | Includes bibliographical references and index. | Audience: Ages 8–11 | Audience: Grades 4–6 | Summary: "Examine a full-color cutaway of a human bone, explore the different ways bones can break, and much more in an amazing augmented reality experience. Learn about the skeletal system in all its disgusting detail"— Provided by publisher.
Identifiers: LCCN 2019049867 (print) | LCCN 2019049868 (ebook) | ISBN 9781541598119 (library binding) | ISBN 9781728414263 (paperback) | ISBN 9781728401300 (ebook)
Subjects: LCSH: Bones—Juvenile literature. | Muscles—Juvenile literature.
Classification: LCC QM101 .O47 2021 (print) | LCC QM101 (ebook) | DDC 611/.71—dc23

LC record available at https://lccn.loc.gov/2019049867
LC ebook record available at https://lccn.loc.gov/2019049868

Manufactured in the United States of America
1-48002-48680-2/24/2020